Dating Sucks

ANDIE M. LONG

Cover design by Tammy Clarke.
Formatting by Tammy Clarke.

INTRODUCTION

When an author starts a new series you can never know how successful it's going to be. I was excited to release The Vampire wants a Wife as I'd had such fun writing it. When it hit number 383 in the whole US Amazon chart I was thrilled. I wrote this book as I was about to release the third book in the series.

I decided to write a short story about how the dating agency came about, with sneak peeks at characters from the three main books, and also to introduce you to Samara who works at the dog grooming salon.

Happy reading!

Andie xo

CHAPTER

One

SHELLEY

I stared at the ticket in my hand and sighed.

WITHERNSEA SINGLES
SPEED DATING NIGHT
22 SEPTEMBER 2016
WITHERNSEA TOWN HALL
Refreshments Included

Had my life really come to this?

Unfortunately, yes. After a year with no dates whatsoever—those who had asked me out were just, well, yuk—I had seen the ad for the speed dating night in the Withernsea Gazette and after the best part of a bottle of wine, I'd called the number on the ad and bought a ticket.

Now I stood outside the venue wondering whether or not I had the confidence to actually go inside the building.

A woman stood at the side of me. Long dark brown hair, brown eyes, slim build but with a decent rack—something I couldn't help but notice given their prominence in her tight red t-shirt. She made me want to run off down the street. If she was the standard of women going in here, then I had bugger all chance of getting a date. "Are you here for the speed dating night?" she asked me.

I nodded. "Yeah, but I'm wondering whether I can actually go through with it."

"With that red hair and porcelain pale skin they'll eat you up. Well, if you're lucky." She winked. "Just look all innocent looking, like a little China doll. You'll get loads of interest."

"Have you been to one of these before?" I asked her.

She nodded. "This is my fourth. I've not found true love, but then I'm not looking for that. I have found quite a few decent shags though. The trouble is they won't let me ask what size dicks the men have which I think is unfair. You can plainly see the size of my boobs; I think they should have to do a hip thrust at the very least."

I was stunned into silence. This woman had no filter.

"I'm Kim." She held out her hand, and I took it in mine and shook. "Come on, I'll take you under my wing. You can sit to the left of me. That way as we rotate I'll have assessed them first. I'll give you a wink or something if they seem okay."

"Excuse me, ladies." A well-to-do male voice said. I only saw him from the back as he brushed past me. I flinched. His hand had been so cold. I watched as the tall man with dark hair disappeared into the building. God, I hoped the heating was on inside. I'd bet he'd walked with how cold he was. Speaking of which, I was still standing outside on a cold, miserable day. It seemed winter was trying to come early this year.

"I guess it's time to go in and give this a shot," I said to Kim. "I'm Shelley, by the way."

Inside the hall there were about forty small tables set in a circle with chairs either side. My mouth dropped open. "Oh my God, I didn't realise there were so many single people in Withernsea."

"Yeah." Kim looked around the gathered crowd, some of whom were drinking their free tea or coffee. "So many sad fuckers."

"Hey, are you saying I'm a sad fucker?" I asked her.

She looked at me, "You came to Withernsea's speed dating night."

"Yeah, you're right, I really am."

She linked her arm through mine. "But the best thing is, that although you'll be lucky to find a mate along this motley crew, you've found a new friend, and you can leave here after the speed dating and get drunk with your new friend at The Marine."

I frowned at her. "And then will you fleece me of all my valuables?"

She cackled. "You're a hoot. We're going to be besties, I just know it. You will have to come meet the gang at Jax's."

"Gang?" Was she trying to co-opt me into some kind of cult?

"Just some friends. Have you been to Jax's? It's a coffee shop and they have the best coffee in the whole damn world. Jax who runs it is lovely."

I breathed a sigh of relief. "Oh, I've heard of it, but I haven't been. I work a lot of hours."

"Oh, what do you do?"

"I'm a buyer for a company. They ask me to get things and I locate them for them."

"You get paid to shop?" Kim's jaw dropped open.

"Well, it's nuts, bolts, pieces of wood, metals, so it's not as exciting as that."

"Oh, pity. Though there aren't many people who can say they buy screws for a living. You wanna say that when these deadbeats ask you what you do for a job. Which they will. They all ask the same dumb questions."

"I don't know why you're here if you're so down on them all already."

"Because some deadbeats have enormous dicks."

I walked over to the refreshment table and picked up a coffee. Kim took it out of my hand and put it back down. "Water only. You don't want coffee breath or stained teeth. Just in case a miracle happens and there's someone here who's actually attractive and has more than one GCSE."

I tilted my head at her. "You are very bitter about the whole dating thing."

"Well, I'm still single, and looking around I don't see that changing anytime soon." She blew her fringe out of her face. "Now, like I said, I'm not looking for a major commitment, but it would be nice to get to know someone a little better. Have more than one date with them. Like a man who could be a male friend and a fuck buddy."

"I think they call those a boyfriend, Kim."

A woman turned on a microphone. It let out a high-pitched scream and a man dropped to the floor clutching his ears. It was the tall, dark haired one again. He had his back to me so I still couldn't see his face.

"We'll keep well away from that weirdo," Kim whispered. "I'll make sure we start at the other side."

"Yes please," I told her.

"So," said the middle-aged woman on the now working microphone. "Welcome to the fifth meeting of Withernsea Speed Dating. I don't know whether to say it's good to see so many familiar faces or whether that's sad because it means you are yet to have found love." She pouted her lips and looked at a few of us like we were wounded puppies.

"Now, just for those who haven't attended before. I'm Daphne and the reason I have set up these events is that I met my husband on a blind date and we've now been very happily married for over thirty years."

"That's not what her husband said to me in bed last week," Kim mumbled.

My eye widened. "You did not?!"

"No I didn't. I don't do married men or old biddies, but your face. Hahahaha."

Jesus, what was this woman on?

"So, if the males could take a seat at one side and we'll get ready to start. Three minutes each, when the bell dings women will move to the right, men stay where you are. Obviously with how many of us there are here tonight you might not meet everyone, but if you could mark on your papers anyone you would like to be in touch with in the future and drop them in this box at the end please. I will email your list of potential dates in the next couple of days. Okay, gentlemen, can you hurry to take your seats now."

"What if you're a man who dates men, or a woman who dates other women?" I asked Kim.

"Tough shit, because this is how she sets it up, so I guess they'd just have to get their gaydar on and suss out potential cock and pussy around the refreshment area."

"Well, I don't think that's exactly in-keeping with the times. There must be a better way to meet people than this?"

"I'm open to suggestions if you can think of any," Kim said. "Until then it's £15 every two weeks to come and sit with these muppets for two hours."

"Ladies, please take your seats." Daphne looked directly at us, and then Kim nodded over to some chairs and I followed her, taking my first seat opposite a guy who couldn't have been over four feet tall.

What a great start.

CHAPTER
Two

THEO

Dating sucked. Especially if you were a 125-year-old vampire.

This was my third attempt at speed dating, but every time I told women I was a vampire they looked at me strangely, went quiet, and never ticked my name on their paper.

I'd had a total of two dates from the previous dating nights. With those I'd not bothered mentioning I was a vampire at all. Unfortunately, they had both ended badly.

The first one wouldn't hold my hand because she said I had a circulation problem. Is it my fault I'm cold?

The second one tried to stick her hand down my trousers. I was appalled. This was not the actions of a lady. She'd then said to me that I owed her £50. I made it clear to her that I was aware of 'women of the night' and that I didn't think she should be soliciting using a speed dating event.

So here I was again hoping it was third time lucky. I was so busy daydreaming I didn't realise I'd knocked into a woman outside the building.

I apologised and moved on. Whoever the two of them were, my shyness stopped me from looking back. Anyway, they weren't necessarily there for the dating evening were they?

Walking inside, I nodded at a few faces I'd seen before and stood away from the refreshment table. I didn't think it was very fair that there was no O-neg available. Not everyone drank tea, coffee, or water. I'd said this to Daphne at the end of the last meeting and she'd just given me a back slap and told me I was hilarious and that women liked a good sense of humour.

I'd been there about fifteen minutes when she switched the microphone on. The noise from it would have made glass shatter had we not got plastic cups, but to my super vampire hearing it felt like the inside of my brain was being scraped out with nails. I dropped to the floor, clutching at my ears until it stopped.

"...if males could take their seats at one side." Here we went again. Let's hope I had better luck this time.

I took my seat opposite an exotic looking woman wearing a black scarf around her head and neck, so you could barely see her face.

The first bell sounded.

"I'm very pleased to meet you. My name is Theo." I held out my hand.

She stared at me without talking for about ten seconds.

Well, this was encouraging.

"I know who you are, darling. The voices are speaking to me. They tell me you will not find your date this evening. The planets have not yet aligned. She is close, but you are not destined to meet tonight."

"Erm, okay. So your name is?"

"My name is Ebony. There is no point in you asking me any further questions because I am not your one. You need to be quiet now and listen to my words. I only came here tonight for you. I was told you would be here, and I had a message to give you."

The little I could see of her face went a grey colour and her eyes rolled in her head. It was most disconcerting.

"Do not attend any more speed dating events. It is a waste of your time. There is a new dating phenomenon coming to Withernsea. Look out for it. It is more in-keeping with modern times, and I am told you are very good with technology?"

"Yes. I have recently developed a social media app for supernaturals. It's called Faceblood."

Her eyes returned to normal.

"I have heard of that. I shall have to look into signing up."

"You believe me? That I'm supernatural? Do you know I'm a vampire?"

"Yes, I know. I'm a Seer. How do you think I am telling you your future? Now I must go because one of my friends is here and she must not see me."

I looked around.

"She is at the opposite end. Now you must

leave, right now. If you don't, you will interfere with Fate and believe me if her plans get messed with, we all suffer. You think PMT is bad. Try PFT."

"PFT?"

"Pissed Fate Temper."

"Oh, well, okay. If you insist, I shall leave here forthwith. Do you have any idea when I will meet my one, just so I can ensure to not book another commitment on that date?"

"Look for the sign."

"Ah, an indication from Fate?"

"No, a sign in Withernsea that says Withernsea Dating Agency."

The bell rang and the woman and I got up.

"This way," she told me, nodding towards a back entrance. "We can slip out without being seen."

I bade her farewell outside the back of the hall and then I made my way back home.

So my one was coming. I just had to wait. Well it had been over a hundred years, what was a little more time?

CHAPTER

Three

SHELLEY

"Hello," I said cautiously, looking over at Kim who had of course sat herself opposite a great looking fair-haired guy.

"Yeah, I'm right here. I know I'm small but you could at least look me in the eyes." The guy in front of me snapped.

I whipped my head straight around to face him but he was a lot lower than I expected and then I had to look down.

He tutted.

"I'm so sorry, I'm new to all this," I told him.

"Yeah, you don't say." The guy eye-rolled me.

What the fuck? For a shrimp he had a massive attitude.

"So I'm Shelley. What's your name?" I asked him.

"It quite clearly says on my name badge that my name is Tristan."

I decided to sit there in silence until the three minutes was up. It was that or lean over and throttle him.

"Well, I'm the leader of the pixies," he said.

"Oh I've not heard of your band, sorry," I replied. "'Fraid I'm out of the loop with the whole music scene. I'd rather watch the TV."

It was as he stomped off that I realised he'd not been sat on the chair, just stood against it. He was even smaller than I'd thought.

I looked across at Kim who wasn't talking to her date anymore either. She gave me a sympathetic smile. "He's a turd. Don't worry about it. He was an a-hole when I talked to him at the last one. You have Johnny coming up and he's nice."

Johnny smiled. "Aww, thank you for saying so."

So did she want a date with him? I didn't want to step on my new friend's toes, but then I guess no one knew who would click with who until the end.

The bell dinged, and we moved on. I took my

seat opposite Johnny. I had a quick look at who I was getting after Kim this time to find a young guy with a LOT of facial hair. Moustache, beard, hairy eyebrows, and his brown hair curled past his shoulders. He had some muscles on him too. But too young for me, I knew that already. I eavesdropped.

"I don't mean to be rude but have your actual bollocks dropped?" Kim asked.

"Hey! I'll have you know I'm eighteen." The guy sat up straighter in his seat.

"Well, you're too young for me. Got an older brother I could have a go at though?"

"I do, but he wants to find a mate."

"That's okay. I can be friends with him if he's attractive enough. With benefits of course."

The guy half-growled. "It's always about Darius. No one ever looks at me properly. It's just 'where's Darius?'"

"Chin up. Once you've got a bit older I'm sure lots of chicks will dig you, but in the meantime tidy up the monobrow and the rest of the facial hair as they need to be able to find you first."

"Kim!" I yelled over.

"Err, you have your own date?" She pointed at Johnny.

Oh shit, yes I did.

I focused on the man in front of me. "I'm so sorry, Johnny. Now you can see why I'm single."

He laughed. "It's fine. I waffle when I'm nervous so expect me to talk bollo… I mean rubbish. See, I already made a fool of myself."

I smiled. Johnny had lovely blue eyes and a light smattering of freckles across his cheeks.

"Well, I guess if we were great at dating we wouldn't be here."

"Speak for yourself," Kim yelled across. "I told you why I come here."

I rolled my eyes at Johnny.

"Your friend's nice," he said. "But I'm not looking for a quickie. I want to date someone and get to know them."

"Me too."

"So what do you do for a living?"

"She buys screws."

"Kim! Can you please concentrate on your own date?"

"He's gone to the loo. No doubt for a nappy change."

"I work as a buyer for a tool company. It's not very exciting but there's plenty of overtime and it pays the bills. How about you?"

"I'm a vet. I love working with animals and to get paid to do it is even better."

"Awww. You save animals lives?"

"Sometimes."

The bell dinged. What a shame as I felt I'd clicked with Johnny. I'd definitely be putting a big fat tick next to his name.

I sat in front of the hairy guy who'd returned from the bathroom with his hair pulled back in a ponytail. It was also obvious that he'd tried to use water to tidy up his eyebrows and tache.

"Hello, I'm Shelley."

"I'm Rhett. Pleased to meet you. Do you come here often?"

"Erm, no. First time."

"Right. And what do you think about women being cougars?"

"It's not my scene, if that was your inference. That I would be your cougar. And FYI I'm only a few years older than you."

"Really? You seem older."

"It's being in here," I told him. "I'm aging rapidly."

"Want to give it up and get slaughtered?" yelled Kim. I looked at her current man, the one I'd be getting next. He was picking his nose.

"Yep. Let's go," I said.

Approaching Daphne, I handed her my paper with Johnny's name ticked. I could only hope. I looked around to see if I could make out if I was missing out on anyone, but there was no one who'd caught my eye. The man who'd fallen to the ground didn't seem to be around. Maybe he'd been taken ill?

"Fuck me. What a bunch of losers. We need a large bottle of wine—each!"

I don't know what it was about my new friend, maybe the fact that she just owned who she was so much, but I liked her immensely already. I didn't really have many friends, being comfortable in my own skin. Maybe I'd got too comfortable? Every evening when I eventually got home it seemed to be a quick bite to eat and a date with the television set. I was estranged from my family. My adoptive parents made it very clear they weren't that keen on my company. My mum had got naturally pregnant with my sister soon after they'd adopted me and that was it, I was no longer good enough.

Yes, I would embrace my new friend, and I would indeed get slaughtered.

Sod it.

We made our way over to The Marine, one of Withernsea's main pubs, and after checking with me, Kim ordered us a bottle of wine and two glasses. Then she got us a corner table. She poured the wine out until it reached about 1mm away from the top of the glass. It was so full I had to lean over and sip a little out of the top.

"Are you a romantic then, Shelley? Looking for your one special person?"

"Yeah, I guess so. Although finding someone who could be special even for a short time would be an improvement on the last year of my life."

"Have you not dated much then lately?"

"I haven't dated at all."

"Excuse me?" Kim put her glass of wine down. "Are you telling me that your pussy hasn't been out trying to eat any leftover sausage?"

"I've not had sex in over a year, no."

"Whoa! I would die if I had that happen to me. Seriously, I need cock every morning and I don't mean for an alarm. You fiddle though, yeah? Get your kicks solo?"

"I'm sorry, I don't play musical instruments. I'm not following."

"Do. You. Masturbate?" Kim yelled. The people at the neighbouring table turned and gave her a look like she was something they'd stood in.

"Oh you know you all do it," she replied to them. "Especially him," I bet. She pointed at the woman's son, who looked about fifteen. "I bet yours has almost fallen off hasn't it, sunbeam?"

"We're leaving," the mother declared. "I told you if we stayed past nine pm they let the riffraff in. Philip, let's go."

"My friend isn't riffraff," I shouted. "She's awesome and for the record yes I do masturbate, and I suggest you do it more often in the hope relaxing makes the stick fall out from up your arse."

"Oh my god, who is this Shelley and where has the one I met an hour or so ago gone?" Kim clutched her sides and gave in to full hearty laughter.

"I'm not as angelic as I look," I told her. "And this wine is going down a little too well."

The rest of the evening passed quickly. I discovered Kim worked in a chemist near to Jax's coffee shop but hated every minute of it.

"It's so boring. Just sitting behind the till or stacking painkillers. I'm surprised I've not taken a load."

"Yes, my job isn't exactly exciting either. If you could do anything what would you do?"

"I'd be a physiotherapist for sports injuries. All those hunky men for me to get my hands on. What about you?"

"I don't know. I've done this job since I left school. I'm not sure I'd be capable of doing anything else."

The landlord shouted time.

"You need to come to Jax's and meet the rest of the gang. When are you free?" Kim asked.

"I'm not working this Saturday? It's a rare day off as it's closed for stocktaking."

"Great. Come to Jax's for eleven am on Saturday and we'll introduce you to her coffee and doughnuts. You'll never want to leave."

My stomach rumbled. "God, I could eat them right now."

"Well, it's not open, but come on, the chippy is only around the corner."

I collapsed into bed that night feeling merry, full, and happy. It was the first true happiness I'd felt in a long time. When I got an email the following night saying Johnny had marked that he'd like to take me on a date, it seemed things were looking up at long last.

CHAPTER

Four

SHELLEY

I'd arranged to meet Johnny at Jetty's, an ice-cream parlour. I figured it was a safe enough choice. Busy, and also I could escape quickly because how long did it take to eat an ice cream?

As I approached the front of the shop, Johnny was just walking over from the other side. He was wearing a camel covered mac which made him look like a pervert. Therefore when he came over to me, hands in the pockets of his mac, it looked like I was meeting a weirdo. If he produced a lollipop or asked if I wanted to see a puppy I was off.

"Good to see you again, Shelley."

"You too. My name's on a Strawberry Sundae so shall we?"

Once inside, we gave our orders to the waitress. I loved Jetty's. It was a little bit corny with its seaside theme and wooden boats on display, but the ice creams were to die for.

Johnny took his pervert mac off to reveal a bright yellow tee and red jeans. He looked like he'd had an accident with mustard and ketchup.

Seriously, he would stop traffic in daylight, mainly because they'd think he was a traffic light.

"So have you lived in Withernsea all your life?" I asked him.

"Yes, born and bred. You?"

"Same."

"Surprised we haven't bumped into each other before then."

"Yeah."

Way to go Shelley, monosyllabic answers. You're bowling him over with your amazing personality.

"So have you had many dates then from the speed dating events?" I asked him.

"A few, but they've not been very successful. I don't think three minutes is enough time to get to know someone enough to make a successful date. Most I've met tell lies. They'll say they work in catering and they mean they're on the counter at McDonald's. They'll say they're single, but they only ditched their boyfriend the day before and he comes and threatens to kick your teeth in. You find out they're highly allergic to cats and yours was sat cuddled into your jumper just before you went out. Dating is a nightmare."

"Yeah, tell me about it. I got so burned by it all that I haven't dated in ages."

"Oh I feel quite honoured then."

"Yeah, you should." I gave out a nervous cackle which made me sound like I'd escaped an asylum.

Thankfully, we were interrupted by the waitress delivering our ice creams.

"Well, it's great to meet someone nice. Well you seem nice anyway, although I know we've only been out for twenty-three minutes. How long do you think is a reasonable amount of dating before marriage by the way?"

I almost choked on a strawberry. "Erm, longer than twenty-three minutes?"

"Oh gosh, I wasn't proposing. See, I told you I was no good at this dating thing. I guess I'm just getting older and I want to know I'm on the same page as people from the off, you know?"

I didn't know. All I wanted was to eat my

goddamn ice cream. Maybe get a good snog on the way home.

"Erm, I guess when you meet the right person and have got to know them and love has kicked in, well, I can't see that being a set time."

"Do you believe in love at first sight?"

I was starting to feel uncomfortable now with this line of questioning. "Not at the moment, but I guess, again, it would have to happen for me to believe it. Or I'd need to know someone who it's happened to."

"Well, I do... because it's happening to me, right now."

Oh fuck. Oh almighty fuck. No, I don't feel the same way. We're just eating ice cream. Help me. Why aren't the portions bigger so I can bury my head in the bowl?

"That woman over there. She's making my heart do funny flips."

My mouth dropped open. I turned to see a woman on her way out of the door. She must have been sat in the back. I didn't know how I'd not noticed her before given her purple and green floral boho style dress that went to her knees. Her hair was a mass of blonde curls. She was a cutie all right. Looking at Johnny's face I could see I'd lost him.

Thank God.

Whoa inner voice where had that come from? This man was very nice, I could do worse. Oh, who was I kidding? He did nothing for me at all. What was happening to him now: his heart going pitter patter, the look on his face, that's what I was looking for happening to me.

"Oh, she's gone."

"Go and get her."

"No." He shook his head. "I'm on a date with you."

"Johnny. You really liked that girl. I don't mind, honestly."

"Really?"

"Go. I'll pay for the ice cream. Go find her."

He took off out of the door. I sat back in my seat. Well what a waste of time that had been. I glanced across. He'd left a chocolate flake on his plate. Not a complete waste of time then. I reached over and snaffled it and stuffed it into my mouth only for him to return and stare at his plate.

"Where's my flake?"

"You left. I didn't want it to go to waste."

"I was just going to give her my number, not abandon our date. Anyway, she's gone. I missed her."

He sat down and looked glumly at his plate.

I called over the waitress. "Can I pay for like five flakes each please? We need to comfort eat."

I said goodbye to Johnny. We agreed not to see each other again. He'd not appealed to me and for the rest of the date he'd spoken about letting the potential love of his life go.

Meanwhile I was back to square one, with no romance in sight. Though if tonight was any indication of my future dating prospects I'd blown it. I decided to walk along the sea front to grab a bit of fresh air before I went home. The sea and the sound of the waves crashing was so relaxing and I felt myself start to unwind. I hadn't even realised how much the tension had been building in my neck and shoulders until my shoulders dropped away from my ears. Surely there was someone out there for me to date? Someone normal? I wondered about joining a dating agency? That might be a possibility. At least I could vet them online first and then make a date when I knew them a little better.

As soon as I got back home, I took my laptop out and typed in the search bar. There was no agency specific to Withernsea but there were a few national sites I'd heard of, so I chose one of those and joined up. Membership complete, I spent the rest of the evening until late working on my profile and then I decided I'd see who chose me.

I went to bed pleased that I'd made an effort and not just let myself hide away back at home.

The next day I was mega busy at work so I didn't have time to check my personal emails. When I got home, I found I had a reply from someone who called himself Stan the Man. For real? I clicked on his photo. Whoa. He was fabulous looking. Dark hair, scruff around his chin, and puppy dog eyes. I read his profile.

Looking for someone with a sense of humour. Well that was me. I'd gone to the speed dating event. That had been hilarious.

Good company.

Okay to take things slow at first.

This was sounding promising…

His message read.

Hey, I'm Stan. You seem a great girl and if you'd like to meet for a drink one night let me know and we can see how it goes.

S.

I typed a reply.

What are you doing tomorrow evening? Meet at The Marine at 8pm?

I left the message and cooked myself a pizza. Once I'd returned to the laptop, I had a new message.

Sounds great. I'll wear a white rose on my lapel so you know who I am. You do the same.

I didn't really understand that seeing as I already knew what he looked like. Believe me, with the usual residents of Withernsea he wouldn't be hard to spot due to the fact that the single women in the area would probably gather round him like he was the new Messiah.

I just typed **okay** and left it at that.

I didn't remember to get a white rose until it was too late. In the end I made one out of toilet tissue. I was beyond caring and if the date went tits up at least I could assemble the pieces back into loo roll and cry into them. I put on a nice jumper and my best black skinny jeans, grabbed my fake leather jacket, and placing my feet into my boots, I called a taxi to take me down to The Marine.

As I exited the car, the wind whistled around my ears and I cursed the fact that I'd let vanity over my hair win out over wearing my woolly hat. I'd bet I'd have earache for days now so this date had better be worth it.

I walked into the pub and looked around. Where was he?

Oh you had to be kidding me.

At a table towards the rear of the bar sat a

man in a mask. A mask looking like the profile picture. Was this another crazy person? Sighing, I walked over to where he sat. He was wearing a white rose on his lapel, a dead one. Great. Way to make an effort. I'd bet it was one he'd had for a previous date and he'd decided to get his money's worth. Tight, and crazy. He took off the mask, and I gasped.

"Oh God, I thought you looked familiar on your photo, but it didn't completely look like you." Tristan the very small man said, or rather grunted.

"Well, it's a makeover shoot photo, but at least I resemble mine unlike yours, you cheating scumbag."

"Do you think I get dates if I'm honest? Do you think people don't go completely on face value? Admit it, you agreed to the date because you thought I was gorgeous."

"But Tristan, you're okay looking anyway. It's your being an arse that gets in the way."

"What?" His eyes widened.

"Can I sit down? I'm not having a date with you but seeing as we're here can I get a drink and sit with you awhile so my evening isn't a total bust?"

"Sitting and drinking with me is kind of a date."

"Well there's going to be nothing beyond my sitting here with a very large glass of wine, so if you'll excuse me, I'm just going to the bar."

Standing in the queue to get my wine, I couldn't believe it. Dating sucked. Totally and utterly sucked.

"Hey, Shelley." A voice came from my left. I turned to find Rav, one of the waiters from my favourite Indian restaurant at my side.

"Rav! Good to see you. They let you out tonight then?"

"Yeah they did, but I have another job and Lucy called a meeting so I'm here with her. He nodded over to a corner where a ginger-haired woman sat.

"You have two jobs? Goodness me, Rav. You're a busy man. What else do you do?" I asked.

"My other job is Hell, simply Hell." He replied. From his expression I figured he didn't really want to talk about it further. He was looking nervously in the direction of his other work colleague.

"Ooh tell me about it. I'm knackered, I've

been run off my feet." I nodded my head. "Anyway, I'd better let you get back to your work mate."

I plonked myself back down in the seat opposite Tristan, or Stan the Man as he was this evening.

"There must be a way of us getting dates we actually want," I sighed.

"Well if there is, I've yet to discover them. Now if we could have less of your constant wittering, what were you saying was wrong with my personality? I'd think you'd be honoured someone of my level wanted to meet you for a date."

I'm not proud of myself for pushing a person of limited stature off a chair, but it was that or throw my drink at him and I needed my alcohol.

After necking the drink at a rapid rate, I legged it from the pub at great speed and called for a taxi to take me home.

I was changing my name to Shelley Haversham, staying at home forever more, I would let the cobwebs gather on my body until someone found me half eaten by rats.

CHAPTER Five

SHELLEY

Saturday morning saw me at Jax's coffee shop. I was actually more excited about this than I had been about my dates! It would be so good to have more friends and maybe I could even have a kind of social life.

I could see Kim sitting with two other women as I pushed open the door of the coffee shop. "Shelley! So glad you made it. Come and let me introduce you to everyone."

I pulled my lips up in a nervous smile.

"We don't bite you know? Come and take a seat." She pulled out the chair next to her, and I took it.

"Right. This is Ebony. She owns the boutique next door. You must go and check out her stock. Her clothes are amazing."

Ebony smiled at me, but her eyes seemed to bore through me. She reached into her handbag and pulled out a small bottle of vodka and placed it on the table next to her coffee. I knew my eyes went wide; I couldn't help it.

Then I noticed the woman next to her. From the back, with her hair up in a ponytail I'd not recognised her, plus she was wearing a pink top and matching slacks, like the sort of outfit dental assistants wore.

It was Johnny's love-of-his-life. The one he'd run out of the ice cream parlour for.

"This is Samara. She owns the dog grooming salon a couple of doors down."

"Hey, Shelley. Great to meet you." She smiled, and it just made her look even prettier. She had fabulous cheekbones with just the right amount of blusher. Pretty and cared for animals. No wonder Johnny had been pulled towards her. She was like a walking cherub. I had no chance when she was around. Plus, a vet and a dog groomer. It was a match made in heaven.

A petite woman with short brown hair came over with a tray of coffees and a plate of chocolate doughnuts.

"And this is Jax, who owns the coffee shop."

"Pleased to meet you, Shelley. What can I get you?"

"Erm. I'll have a latte please and one of those fabulous looking doughnuts."

"Oh there's already one of those for you on the plate. Kim insists you try one." Jax laughed.

"We apologise for Kim's behaviour at the speed dating event," Samara said.

"You weren't there so how can you apologise when you don't even know what I did?"

"Because it's you, Kim. There's no way you didn't do anything naughty."

"She was okay actually. Rescued me from a fate worse than death. It was truly hideous. There was no one there worth dating."

"Actually, your future husband was there, but it wasn't the right time for you to meet, so it didn't happen," Ebony said.

Everyone sat there in silence for a few moments.

"You'll have to excuse, Ebony. She comes out with these random things. She thinks she's psychic, but she won't give up the winning lottery numbers so I'm not buying it," Kim giggled.

"You'll find out soon enough yourself." Ebony turned to look at her. "You won't find it so amusing when the police officer gets you."

"That's a regular Friday night, Ebony, for me. It's the cuffs. Gets me every time." She winked.

Ebony took the top off the vodka and took a large swig. "It's the visions. I get a migraine if I don't drink," She explained.

I nodded. I found myself with a complete lack of words.

Despite the occasional weird conversation, I found the women to be a great group and felt instantly at home with them. We chatted about our jobs and lack of love lives. Every one of us was single.

"Hey, have you heard who's renting out the office space above you yet, Ebony?" Kim asked. She turned to me. "It was a photography place but everyone's gone digital so they left."

"It will have a new purpose very, VERY, soon," Ebony said and she once again stared at me. "Are you happy in your job, Shelley?"

I sighed. "Not really. I like the buzz I get when the company is pleased with what I bought them and the price I got, but it's not very fulfilling buying tools."

"Hmmm," she said. "So, you like matching things; you've had the worst experiences with dating agencies which around here are sadly lacking; and there is vacant office space above my shop, available for rent at a decent price. Coincidence?"

"You could totally run your own dating agency and I could be your assistant!" Kim half yelled. "Oh my God, this is the most amazing idea ever."

"I'd sign up," said Samara.

"And me," added Jax.

Various other customers around the coffee shop shouted up. "We'd join."

I sat back stupefied. Could I do this? Set up my own agency?

"It's still kinda matching buyers with screws if you think about it." Kim guffawed.

I took a bite out of a chocolate doughnut, the first chance I'd had to try it due to our constant talking.

"Oh my fucking good God." I almost orgasmed in my seat as the chocolate goodness hit home. "This doughnut."

"You'd be within spitting distance of those doughnuts if you rented Ebony's upstairs." Kim elbowed me.

I chewed on my lip. I had some savings because I'd had nothing else to do with my money other than save it.

"How long would I need to take the lease for?" I asked Ebony.

"I'll leave it open-ended, because I already know that you aren't going to leave there for a long time. It's going to be one of the most successful dating agencies in England."

Oh-kay then. Perhaps I should have known better than to ask.

"I'll crunch some figures when I get home. Kim, you'd better tell me your current rate of pay so I can see what I could pay you. I might have to start off alone though."

"No!" Ebony said firmly. "You will need Kim from the beginning. You are going to be run off your feet with applications as soon as news of your first match gets out. Now drink your coffee and I will show you your new offices."

I found this woman unnerving. You could almost believe she was telling the truth.

"Can I be your guinea pig?" Samara asked.

"I'd really love to find love. It's kind of essential to my wellbeing and I've been on a bit of a downer lately. I can see this is going to be so good for all of us."

"You sure can. I'll put together an application form and stuff. Oh my god, I'm getting excited."

Jax pulled up a chair. "We are so Girl Bosses. We should meet up once a month as a collective. I got it! We'll call ourselves *Female Entrepreneurs do it with their colleagues*."

I opened my mouth to protest about the name, but Kim gave me a warning side-eye and said. "Jax, that's a fantastic idea. We'll leave you to sort the details out."

"Yay!" She clapped her hands together. "I'll have t-shirts printed for us and everything."

She went off back to the counter and Kim turned to me.

"We don't upset the provider of coffee and cake." She warned me.

She had a point.

I said goodbye to everyone and went home where I spent the rest of the weekend working my arse off putting together a business plan and researching everything I could on the internet.

By the time Monday morning came around I could barely keep my eyes open. I believed it was only adrenaline from the excitement about it all keeping me going. I had contacted someone about setting me up a computer system and had drawn up the preliminary forms for applicants.

On Monday, I booked a couple of days annual leave. Tuesday afternoon, I had an appointment with the bank who approved my loan for Withernsea Dating. I also left with the names and telephone numbers of four members of staff including the man who'd approved my loan.

On Wednesday, I returned to the coffee shop where I signed a lease with Ebony for rental of the offices above her boutique. I met with Samara for a coffee (and of course a chocolate doughnut) and I got her to complete an application form.

"You understand that at the beginning I won't have many people to choose from?" I told her.

"Oh, I don't think that will be the case for long, but yes. I understand. Happy to be the tester."

When I got home, I called Johnny.

"Hey, Johnny. I set up a new business and I think you might want to be my first male applicant…"

CHAPTER

Six

SHELLEY

I was working weekends at the agency while we got established and I worked my notice at the tool company. I'd handed in my notice within an hour of opening the agency, as word of mouth flew around Withernsea. Well, actually word of Kim who was like a gob on a stick. She'd walked around Withernsea sea front with flyers and accosted anyone on their own. The subscriptions meant I knew we would have our wages covered for at least the first month and for a newly opening business that was something.

I sent Johnny out with Samara on the test date, and…

They came home engaged.

You heard me. ENGAGED.

They stormed into the office the next morning.

Samara was grinning from ear to ear and Johnny couldn't stop staring at her, a look of love and idolisation on his face.

"Shelley. Good news!" She beamed.

I smiled. "Well, it looks like the date went well?"

"We're engaged!" She held out a hand flashing an enormous diamond. "We just clicked, immediately! I feel like I've known him all my life."

"We are just perfect together in every way," Johnny said.

And then they both blushed due to the innuendo of his statement.

"Well, I'm… so happy for you." I rushed over and hugged them. Internally, I felt like they were off their tiny heads but who was I to argue with my dating agency matchmaking formula. I'd worked with the IT expert and between us we had come out with the perfect system. I was a natural at matchmaking. My first match had created an engagement already!

"Yeah, is that the Withernsea Gazette? I've got the perfect story for you. Couple fall instantly in love due to being matched by a dating agency computer. You can come at three pm. That's great. Thank you."

I watched as Kim put the phone down. "Samara, you okay with showing off that ring some more?"

"Absolutely. Shelley has done me the most wonderful service. She has no idea how grateful I am to her."

She grabbed her husband-to-be's arm. "Let's go, leave these busy business people to it." She turned back around to me. "We're going home now but we'll be back at three."

They left the office.

"They are totally going home to have sex. I hate them. They are far too happy. Is this what we have to do now? Put up with all these happy loved up faces in Withernsea?"

"We get paid for it." I shrugged. "And according to Ebony, our husbands are on their way."

"Course they are. She's had one too many vodkas that one."

"Single women running a matchmaking agency. We find love for others but not for us." I sighed.

CHAPTER

Seven

SAMARA

Shelley simply had no idea what she'd done for me.

And she never would.

You see, I was Cupid. Well, the Cupid for Withernsea. The idea of one cupid with a bow and arrow for the whole world, well that was an entirely unrealistic proposition.

Anyway, I'd been sent here under the guise of being an animal groomer and… I'd got a little down and depressed and neglected my duties somewhat.

That had meant the singles of Withernsea had been wandering around lonely and with no focus for a year or so.

But all I had needed was to find love myself!

As soon as I'd met Johnny in The Marine, I

just knew that he was my one. But I'd 'accidentally' given him the equivalent of a needlestick injury with my arrow just to be sure.

Now we were to be married, and love could once again avail itself in Withernsea.

But I thought I could sit back and relax for a while longer.

Because Cupid didn't need to work while Shelley Linley was around, did she? I could always work my magic now and again to help things along.

But the rest of the time, I'd just focus on keeping the animals of Withernsea looking their best, my fiancé could keep them healthy, and we could plan our own happy ever after!

CHAPTER

Eight

THEO

One year later…

I'd decided to have a wander around Withernsea this evening because, well to be honest, I was bored. I'd spent most of the last year in my home working on my Faceblood app and being miserable, only rousing myself for my weekly cards night with my friends. I'd given up on love. There had been no sign like Ebony had told me there would be.

I took myself for a stroll to see if anything had changed in the town and decided to take a left at the chemist shop. I'd never been down here before. There was a block of shops containing Jax's, (what a shame I didn't drink coffee, I'd heard such great things about it). Then I saw the sign above the boutique.

WITHERNSEA DATING AGENCY
Find your ideal partner
www.withernseadating.com

A woman opened the door of the boutique and stepped outside, wobbling a little as she did so. I dashed over to steady her, forgetting I wasn't supposed to use my super-speed in public.

"Thank you," she said, and I recognised her voice from the speed dating event. "Now go home and fill out an application."

"How do you know I'm consider—"

"The vampire wants a wife," she replied, and she winked at me.

THE END

ABOUT THE AUTHOR

Andie M. Long lives in Sheffield with her son and long-suffering partner.

When not being partner, mother, or writer, she can usually be found on Facebook or walking her whippet, Bella.

FOLLOW ME ON FACEBOOK
Andie M. Long

AND INSTAGRAM
@andieandangelbooks

THE PARANORMALS

Hex Factor

Heavy Souls

We Wolf Rock You

Satyrday Night Fever

Fright Wedding

SUCKING DEAD

Suck My Life